LEGO NINJAGO
MASTERS OF SPINJITZU

NINJA vs. NINJA

ADAPTED BY KATE HOWARD

SCHOLASTIC INC.

ISBN 978-0-545-82552-8

LEGO, the LEGO logo, NINJAGO, the Brick and Knob configurations and the Minifigure are trademarks of the LEGO Group. © 2015 The LEGO Group. Produced by Scholastic Inc. under license from the LEGO Group. Published by Scholastic Inc. SCHOLASTIC and associated logos are trademarks and/or registered trademarks of Scholastic Inc.

12 11 10 9 8 7 6 5 4 3 2 1   15 16 17 18 19/0

Printed in the U.S.A.   40
First printing, May 2015

A DESPERATE SEARCH

Zane had been missing for many months. The Ninja of Ice was being held prisoner on Master Chen's secret island.

Cole, Jay, Kai, and Lloyd knew Zane was on the island somewhere. So when Chen invited them to take part in his Tournament of Elements, they went to search for their missing friend. But first, they had to fight in the tournament.

Inside his prison cell, Zane had forgotten who he was. "Where am I?"

"You're in danger, Zane. You have to get out o here," a familiar voice replied.

"Who are you?" Zane asked.

"I'm a friend," said Pixal. Her voice came from the cell next to Zane's. "You're a Nindroid—a ninja. Your friends have come to save you. But they can't do it all . . . You have to fight."

As Zane tried to remember, the other ninja prepared for their next battle. They were eating breakfast in the cafeteria at Master Chen's palace.

"This isn't just a fighting tournament," Lloyd told Cole, Jay, and Kai. "It's a way for Chen to steal all the Elemental Masters' powers. But we still don't know why."

"And we still don't know where Zane is," Jay said. "Which is why we all need to win our first rounds—so we'll have more time."

Master Chen's voice rang out over the loudspeaker. "Would the following Masters please go to their assigned arenas: Speed, Gravity, Smoke, Nature, Mind, and . . . Fire!"

Kai gulped. It was his turn for battle!

"And remember," said Chen, "only one can remain!"

THE BATTLES BEGIN

The day's first battle was between Turner, Master of Speed, and Gravis, Master of Gravity. Their arena was a cherry blossom tree growing from the ledge of a cliff.

A Jade Blade was perched at the top of the tree. Whichever Master reached the Blade first would be declared the winner.

"Fight!" Master Chen shouted, and the Elemental Masters began their battle.

Turner zipped around the tree. When he slowed down, Gravis plucked flowers and tossed them at his opponent. Then the Master of Gravity used his powers to pull the Jade Blade toward him.

Suddenly, the Master of Speed leaped out of nowhere and snagged the Blade!

"Winner!" Chen cried, pointing at Turner. "Lo-ser!" He giggled as Gravis disappeared through a trapdoor.

The second battle was between Neuro,
Master of Mind, and Bolobo, Master of Nature.
The Jade Blade they were competing for was
at the top of a jagged boulder.

At first, the two men just stood there, staring
at each other.

"They call this a fight?" Lloyd asked.

"Wait for it," said Sensei Garmadon.

Suddenly, Neuro began to read Bolobo's mind. When Bolobo made giant roots crawl out of the ground, Neuro was one step ahead.

"Never underestimate the power of the mind," said Garmadon.

But Bolobo kept shooting vines at Neuro. The Master of Nature attacked so quickly, Neuro couldn't keep up. Soon, the Master of Mind was all tied up.

"I didn't see that coming," Neuro said.

But the battle wasn't over. Neuro's mental power soon overpowered Bolobo again. Using his opponent's vines to climb up the rock face, the Master of Mind grabbed the Jade Blade.

"Winner!" Master Chen cried. To Bolobo, he sang, "Lo-ser!"

A trapdoor appeared in the ground, and Bolobo disappeared.

FIRE VS. SMOKE

The final battle was Kai, Master of Fire, versus Ash, Master of Smoke. Kai knew he had to get to the Jade Blade first. If he didn't, that would be the end of his search for Zane.

Kai stood before a wooden bridge stretching over the mouth of a volcano. On Master Chen's command, the battle began!

Kai and Ash raced toward the Jade Blade. As he ran, Ash used his powers to flip the bridge over. The Jade Blade fell toward the steaming lava. It landed on a small ledge far below the two competitors.

From the audience, Lloyed shouted, "C'mon, Kai—use your power!"

Ninjaaaago! Kai whirled into a Spinjitzu tornado.

The battle raged on. The two Elemental Masters leaped from perch to perch, avoiding the lava. Every time Kai got close to the Jade Blade, Ash was there, too.

Kai shot fire at Ash. Ash escaped into a puff of smoke. Kai jumped toward the Jade Blade— and grabbed it!

"Winner!" Master Chen cried. "Lo-ser!" Chen pushed a button on his throne, and Ash disappeared.

Later, Master Chen stood before the three losers in his underground temple. He used his staff to absorb their elemental powers.

Clouse whispered in his master's ear. "Let me use my sorcery to put an end to the ninja."

Master Chen chuckled. "We'll use your magic in time, Clouse. But not when there are other ways. It's time to switch things up!"

NINJA VS. NINJA

"No!" Cole shouted. He stared at a list on the palace wall. "Chen can't do this."

"Why does it say I have to fight Cole?" Jay said "It didn't say that before!"

Clouse walked over. "Is there a problem, ninja?"

"You changed the brackets," Kai growled.

Clouse just shrugged. "Oopsie."

"The fight isn't until tonight. We have time to figure out what Chen's up to," Lloyd said.

"I know someone who can help . . ." Kai said.

"We need your help, Neuro," Lloyd begged the Master of the Mind.

Neuro focused on the ninja's thoughts. "You think I can get close to Chen to read his mind, so you can find your robotic friend, Zane, and then you won't have to fight."

"Why should I help you?" Neuro asked. "The sooner you're out, the better for me."

"Look into my head and you'll see what this tournament is really about." Lloyd focused his thoughts on Chen stealing everyone's powers. "It's only a matter of time before Chen steals your power, too. Are you in?"

Neuro nodded.

Later that day, while Jay and Cole prepared for battle, the other ninja tracked down Neuro again.

"Did you see into Chen's head?" Kai asked.

"I'm sorry," Neuro said. "I couldn't get past Clouse. But I did see something inside his mind. The powers Chen are collecting are for a spell."

IN THE ARENA

Cole and Jay squabbled sometimes—especially over Nya, Kai's sister. But they were still teammates. And friends.

"This fight's been a long time coming," said Cole.

Lloyd shook his head. "We don't have control over *who* we fight, but we do have control over *how* we fight. Jay's not your enemy—Chen is."

"Let the battle begin!" Chen cried.

Jay and Cole rushed into the battle arena.
Jay threw an arc of lightning across the arena,
just missing Cole. Then Cole used his powers to
explode the ground beneath Jay's feet.

"Is that all you've got?!" Jay hissed.

Chen giggled. "Clouse, go get me popcorn.
This is turning out better than I expected."

HELP FROM AN OLD FRIEND

Meanwhile, Zane was trying to escape from his prison cell. He tugged at his chains.

From the next cell, Pixal reminded him, "Zane, you're built differently. You have to search deep within yourself . . ."

Zane looked down at his hands. Suddenly, his arm opened and hidden blades slid out!

"Hurry, Zane," Pixal urged.

Zane sliced off his shackles. Then he began to grind through the bars between his cell and Pixal's. "Let's get out of here."

He stopped short inside Pixal's cell. "Pixal, you're . . . you're . . ."

Pixal's voice came out of a computer screen. "Scrapped."

She was no longer a Nindroid—she was just a heap of spare parts!

"Zane, you must go on alone," Pixal's voice said. "Find your friends. Stop Chen. Don't worry about me . . . I will always be a part of you."

"You're right," Zane said. He reached into the computer and pulled out a small chip. "You will always be a part of me."

Zane pressed the chip into his central processor. Pixal came back to life inside Zane's head!

"Zane, you're ingenious!" Pixal said.

"Upgraded," Zane said happily. "Let's both get out of here."

Suddenly, warning lights flashed inside Zane's head. "Zane, behind you!"

Zane turned. It was Clouse!

Zap! Clouse hit Zane with a Taser. Everything went black.

A FRIENDLY FACE-OFF

Back in the arena, Jay and Cole were still locked in a bitter face-off.

"I'm stronger than you thought, eh?" Jay taunted.

Cole lashed out, tossing Jay aside. As Jay crashed to the dirt, Cole froze.

"What are we doing?" Cole stared at his fallen friend. "I don't want you out. You're not my enemy, Chen is."

Jay nodded. "We used to be good friends—"

"The best, right?" blurted out Cole.

"How are we supposed to stop fighting?" Jay asked. "We can't both win."

Cole glanced at Chen. "Maybe we can draw it out until they call a tie. Quick—attack me! But not hard."

"What is this, patty-cake? I'm bored!" Master Chen cried.

"Release the blade chariots!" Master Chen cried. A gate opened, and three huge vehicles blasted into the arena.

"I got your back," Cole promised Jay.

"And I've got yours!" Jay replied.

Ninjaaaa-go! Together, the two ninja were more than the chariots could handle. One by one, Cole and Jay took the chariots down!

"Enough!" Chen hollered. "If neither of you will win, then both of you will lose!" He jabbed at buttons on his control panel.

Trapdoors began to open all over the floor. Jay and Cole had to leap and dodge to keep from falling into Chen's dungeon.

"We can't both lose," Cole told Jay. "Chen's right. There can only be one."

Jay nodded. "It should be you. You take the Jade Blade."

Cole grabbed the Blade . . . and threw it to Jay!

"Winner!" Chen declared. "Master of Lightning moves on."

Cole smiled. "Win this thing, Jay."

Before Jay could reply, Chen punched one final button, and Cole fell through a trapdoor. He was out of the competition.

"About time," Chen whined. "Jeesh."

Clouse glared at the other ninja. "And then there were three."

"Cole may be gone, but he did not lose. Let what he did here today be a lesson for us all: Know thy enemy, but more important, know thy friend," Sensei Garmadon told the ninja.

The ninja would never give up on one another. And there were others who would not give up on them, either . . .

Back in Ninjago, Nya was searching for her brother and the rest of the team.

As she drove across a sand dune, Zane's falcon appeared. The falcon squawked, alerting Nya to a beacon on her radar.

"That's Zane's beacon coming from off the coast!" She gasped. "Sensei Wu, come in . . . Do you read? I may have found the ninja!"